Sweet Child, Don't Be Afraid

Sweet Child, Don’t Be Afraid

ISBN 979-8-9906553-9-3

This Book Belongs To:

....

A Note to Parents

If your little one has ever been afraid at night, you are not alone. I've been through this stage too. When the lights go out, imagination can grow big. Shadows feel larger. Rooms feel different. When everything gets quiet, little hearts can start to feel unsure.

In those moments, our children don't need big explanations. They need us.

Stay close. Speak gently. Keep the routine steady. Sit on the bed a little longer if needed. Pray with them. Remind them softly:

You are safe. I am here. God is near.

I hope this book brings comfort to your child – and a little encouragement to you, too.

Whitney

Sweet Child, Don't Be Afraid

Whitney Ramos

For every child that's ever been afraid at nighttime.

Sweet child, don't be afraid,

When night feels different from the day.

From sunrise to sunset the day
fades away,

Now bedtime has come at the end
of the day.

When lights go out and shadows grow,

And quietness fills the room just so.

The small toys look tall and wide,

My dark bedroom seems bigger inside.

Your room is
still your room
at night,

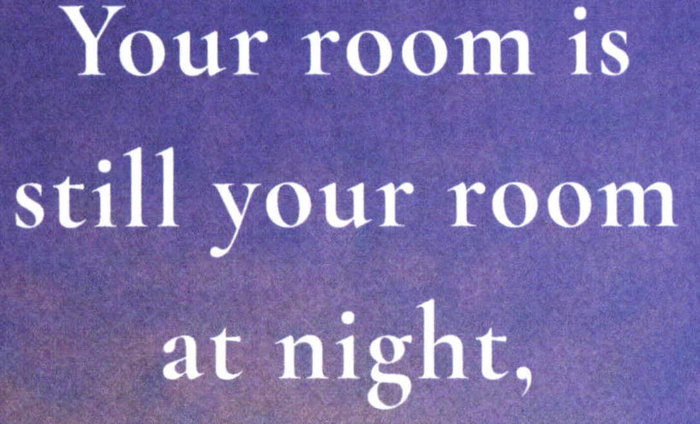

A very safe place
in the morning
light.

Sweet child, close your tired eyes.
Let gentle dreams begin to rise.

You don’t have to shout or fight.

You don’t have to win the night.

Just whisper soft, as brave kids do,

"Jesus, I am safe with You."

And in His name, be still and rest –

And let His peace settle in your chest.

For morning always comes again.
And light will fill your room –
amen.

My sweet child, don’t be afraid,
even in the quiet dark,
God is near.

Goodnight, my sweet child,

Sweet dreams.

The End

"In peace I will lie down and sleep, for You alone, Lord, make me dwell in safety."

Psalm 4:8

A Bedtime Prayer

Dear God,
Thank You for loving me.
Please keep me safe tonight.
In Jesus' name,
Amen.

About the Author

Whitney loves Jesus and loves children.
She writes faith-filled stories to bring
comfort, courage, and peace to little hearts.

Sweet dreams.

www.ingramcontent.com/pod-product-compliance
Lightning Source LLC
LaVergne TN
LVHW070224110826
845147LV00003B/641

* 9 7 9 8 9 9 0 6 5 5 3 9 3 *